Amelia's Itchy ~ Twitchy, LOVEY ~ DOVEY SUMMER AT CAMP MOSQUITO

by Marissa Moss

(and the camper in Cabin 5, amelia!)

Simon & Schuster Books for Young Readers

New York   London   Toronto   Sydney

This notebook is dedicated to
Mollie Katzen,

wishing her the best summer ever!

SIMON & SCHUSTER BOOKS FOR YOUNG READERS
An imprint of Simon & Schuster Children's Publishing Division
1230 Avenue of the Americas, New York, New York 10020
Copyright © 2008 by Marissa Moss

All rights reserved, including the right of reproduction in whole
or in part in any form.

SIMON & SCHUSTER BOOKS FOR YOUNG READERS
IS A TRADEMARK OF SIMON & SCHUSTER, INC.

Amelia® and the notebook design are
registered trademarks of Marissa Moss.

Thanks,
Paula! → A Paula Wiseman Book
Book design by Amelia
(with help from Lucy Ruth Cummins)
The text for this book is hand-lettered. ↙   And it took
almost a
WHOLE
summer!
Manufactured in China
2   4   6   8   10   9   7   5   3

CIP data for this book is available
from the Library of Congress.

ISBN-13: 978-1-4169-4722-6
ISBN-10: 1-4169-4722-1

Summer is supposed to be a lazy time, a time to do NOTHING. At least, that's what I think. Mom has other plans. She wants me to go to Camp Runamucka. I told her no way. I told her I'd rather spend the summer in boiling hot Chicago with my dad, stepmom, and half brother. I told her I'd even rather go there with Cleo, the most annoying sister ever, so that shows how much I <u>don't</u> want to go to camp.

Unfortunately, Mom doesn't care what I think.

Don't you realize what a great opportunity this is for you? You're going to have so much FUN!

I never got to go to camp when I was a kid. I hope you know how lucky you are, young lady.

There are three things wrong with what she says.

Wrong Thing #1: Whenever someone <u>tells</u> you how much fun you'll have, you'd better watch out! If you need convincing, if they have to spell it out, how much fun could it be?

mom lost her credibility on that front a long time ago.

It'll be fun to visit Uncle Myron. You can go through his amazing collection of National Geographic magazines!

It's fun going to the dentist — you even get to pick a prize!

Why don't you enter that essay contest? It'll be FUN!

The grown-up definition of "fun" isn't fun for kids — it's "you'd better have fun because I'm making you do this whether you like it or not."

Wrong Thing #2: When a parent tells you how tough they had it when they were a kid, it's always a bad sign. It means they expect you to be deeply grateful for some ordinary thing that's no big deal to anyone normal, but it is to the parent.

Do you know how fortunate you are to have the luxury of a toilet - a TOILET!? With soft, cushy toilet paper, no less! I didn't have a toilet. I had an outhouse full of big, icky spiders. Would you like to use an outhouse? I don't think so!!

Wrong Thing #3: When a grown-up asks "Do you know how lucky you are?" they don't want an answer. They want you to agree to whatever they say to prove that you're not an ungrateful brat. There's no good answer to this. If you say yes, you've given in to whatever they want you to do. If you say no, they'll force you to do it anyway to teach you not to be such a spoiled, greedy child.

You're right— I should be thankful I have clothes to wear, that I don't have to run around naked and freeze my tush off. Plus be embarrassed.

But does it have to be these clothes? I'd be even more grateful if I could wear something at least half-way cool.

Think how appreciative I'd be to wear something that actually fit.

Something that's in style, not an old hand-me-down from a decade ago.

But the MOST wrong thing is that I don't want to go! What if the other girls in my cabin torment me? What if the counselors are ex-prison guards? What if the food is worse than cafeteria food? (Is that possible?) And if I'm gone, I'll miss those things that make summer <u>summer</u> — doing nothing, reading the same comic books over and over again, going to the pool with friends — those are too important to miss. If I don't do them, will I still feel like I've <u>had</u> a summer or will I feel cheated?

WHAT MAKES SUMMER SUMMER

If these things don't happen, have you really had a summer vacation?

① You get an interesting tan line.

Wow! It looks like I'm wearing a T-shirt and shorts even when I'm not!

② You read a really long book you never thought you'd finish.

③ You eat ice cream three times in one day.

④ You invent a new kind of dive at the pool.

⑤ You spend the entire day in your pajamas. Why bother to get dressed?

Ah, this is the life — nowhere to go, nothing to do!

And NO homework!

It's true you can do some of these things at camp — actually most of them. But you can't do the last one and that's the most important one, not having to do ANYTHING at all - even getting dressed.

I was ready to fight Mom on this one. She can't <u>make</u> me have fun. I mean, there's no such thing as Forced Fun. But then she said something that blew away all my arguments.

And the best part is Carly is going too!

I talked to her parents and it's all set. You'll take the bus together, be in the same cabin, the same group!

If my best friend is going, that makes a BIG difference. Then it really could be fun. Then it's her and me — away from our families. What could be better than that? I called Carly right away so we could make plans.

me ↓

Mom said you're going to Camp Runamucka with me. It'll be GREAT!

Yeah! I read the brochure and we can ride horses and canoe and learn archery and all kinds of cool stuff!

Carly ↓

A summer of no Cleo and lots of Carly — that sounds terrific! So now I'm excited about camp, but I can't let Mom know that. I have to slowly, grudgingly give in. Otherwise she'll think that she really does know what's fun for me when she still doesn't have a clue. Even when she's right, I can't agree with her so quickly or she'll get the wrong idea — the wrong idea being she knows what's best for me, not me.

I've used this strategy before when Mom wanted me to take guitar lessons and at first I really didn't want to, but then I decided it would be cool to learn to play "Stairway to Heaven." I didn't want Mom to think she could change my mind so easily, so I slowly morphed into agreeing with her.

① First I told her I'd go to a lesson if I didn't have to take out the trash for a month.

I'll be losing a half hour of my precious time for the lesson...

...plus taking time to practice, so I should have some way to get back my lost free time.

No trash chore for a month buys back a little of that time. Is it a deal?

That worked great because I seemed reluctant about the lessons PLUS I got out of trash duty.

② Then I pretended going to guitar was like going to the doctor's for a shot. On the ride to and from the lesson, I said hardly anything.

me, scowling and slouching →

What are you playing now?

← Mom would act all nice and chatty while I glared out the window in as LOUD a silence as I could make. But I wouldn't argue or yell. That part was over.

③ Then eventually I acted like it was totally normal to go to guitar. Mom couldn't stop smiling.

I'm SO glad you're getting something out of these lessons. It's a good thing I made you do it — think how proud you'll be when you can play!

yeah.

The key is NOT to be enthusiastic about it — keep your tone neutral.

I'll do something like that for summer camp — a gradual softening of attitude so Mom thinks she's convinced me of something. I used to be more stubborn about these things. If I started out disagreeing with Mom, I could NEVER admit she was right even when I figured out later that she was. Now I'm better about that, but I still need a slow change, not a quick shift, or I feel like I'm giving in too much.

There's a way to grade this kind of stubborness. I call it the Measure of Muleness. I used to fall in the Hard as Rock category, but now I'm much better.

Hmmph! I call stubborn mules "teenagers." You know the expression — "stubborn as a teenager!"

MEASURE OF MULENESS
(OR MULISHNESS)

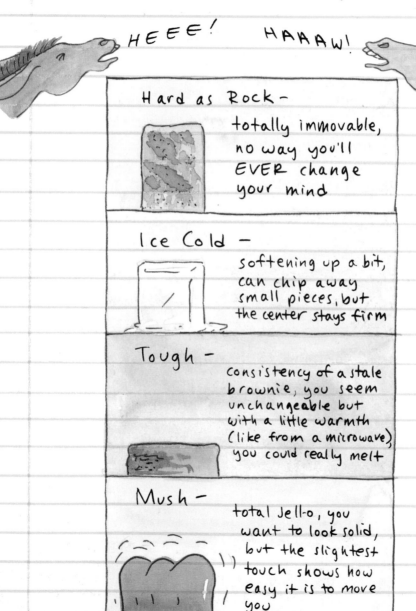

HEEE!   HAAAW!

Hard as Rock — totally immovable, no way you'll EVER change your mind

Ice Cold — softening up a bit, can chip away small pieces, but the center stays firm

Tough — consistency of a stale brownie, you seem unchangeable but with a little warmth (like from a microwave) you could really melt

Mush — total Jell-o, you want to look solid, but the slightest touch shows how easy it is to move you

I'm about at the stale brownie stage now, almost chewable. I told Mom as long as she gives me lots of Bug-Off to pack, I'll go to camp. And maybe I need a snakebite kit and some mousetraps too.

Carly made a great list of absolutely essential equipment we <u>have</u> to bring to camp. Unfortunately, her list and Mom's are total opposites — except they both include clothes and flip-flops.

↙ Carly's To-Pack List   Mom's To-Pack List ↘

Carly's To-Pack List	Mom's To-Pack List
nail polish (3 different colors for a change of pace)	underwear
books and magazines	socks
flip flops	shorts
sketchbook or notebook	T-shirts
pens and pencils	sweatshirt
tiny flashlight	jeans
candy	toothpaste, floss, toothbrush
junk food	shampoo, soap
clothes	pj's
bathroom stuff	bathing suit
binoculars	sunblock
telescope	bug spray
bikini	flip-flops
big beach towel	hairbrush
sunglasses	stamps for letters home
lip gloss	

This ALL sounds good!

There's NOTHING fun about this list!

Any list that starts with underwear CAN'T be good!

I just combined the two lists and Mom actually said yes to everything — except the telescope and binoculars because she's afraid they'll get stolen or broken. I was really beginning to get excited about camp.

Then Mom said:

I panicked! Going to the same school as Cleo was bad enough, but going to the same camp! That was unsurvivable! First I was upset. Then I was furious.

I couldn't help but think of the time Cleo went on the science field trip with my class — it was MY MOST EMBARRASSING MOMENT EVER!

Cleo didn't see what the problem was. She thought it was fine for us to go together.

I'm taking the counselor-in-training course so I can work at summer camps. I'm not really in camp at all.

What's the big deal? I'll be with the older kids — far away from the little kids like you.

I bet we'll never even see each other.

Mom said Cleo was right and I should stop acting like a baby. I was still mad, but when I told Carly about it, she said the same thing. She tried to convince me we'd still have fun.

"Who cares about Cleo?" she said. "She won't be in our cabin or our group. We won't even eat meals at the same time, I bet. It'll be like she's on another planet."

I wanted to believe her. "I guess you're right," I said. Really, I _hoped_ she was right, but I had a sinking feeling she was wrong, wrong, wrong.

I have to give Cleo some credit, though. When it was time to take the bus to camp, she didn't even try to sit next to me. She sat in the back with some other kids she knew. I sat next to Carly and I could almost pretend Cleo wasn't on the bus at all — just me and my best friend, going away together.

Which would have been great except we were going away in the smelliest, grossest way possible — on the camp bus. We tried to find a good seat, meaning one that wasn't sticky, didn't have gum on the back of it, and was next to a window that actually opened.

Seats in the front are the smelliest because that's where the bus fumes are the strongest.

← Seats in the far back mean you get out last — no one wants that!

↑ Seats in the middle are the bumpiest — you practically hit your head on the ceiling every time the bus hits a pothole.

We ended up somewhere between the middle and the front, but nothing could save us from the singing that filled the whole bus. For some reason, teachers and camp counselors think that singing stupid songs makes a long drive seem shorter. Really it's the other way around — you can't believe you'll have to listen to another chorus of 99 Bottles of Beer on the Wall and yet you do. There's always time for another round.

...you take one down and pass it around...

By the time the bus pulled into camp, Carly and I were ready to jump out the window.

We needed fresh air! We needed to get off our sore rear ends and we needed a break from off-key singing!

After the torment of the bus ride, the camp looks great. It isn't smelly, crowded, or noisy. And there are no mean kids in my cabin — at least that I can tell. One girl, Kayla, is too busy crying from homesickness to have the energy to be mean. She hasn't been gone for even one whole day and already she misses everyone and everything at home really, really badly. If she's this sad now, what will she be like after a week?

The other girls try to make Kayla feel better, and our counselors are being extra, extra sweet to her.

Paris — she's a master of long, involved jokes that are HILARIOUS!

Miri — she's on the swim team back home and plans to spend as much time in the water as possible.

Kayla →

I feel bad for her, but I wonder what's at home that's good enough to cry this many tears over.

Yuki — she's very shy. She's barely said two words yet — and she didn't sing on the bus.

Each cabin has two counselors. Ours are Crystal and Jolene. Crystal isn't a real name, it's a "spirit" name, whatever that means.

← Crystal aka Lorraine

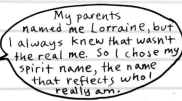

My parents named me Lorraine, but I always knew that wasn't the real me. So I chose my spirit name, the name that reflects who I really am.

Layla — she's crazy about horses and wears riding boots all the time.

Crystal is also big on aromatherapy and astrology. She took roll by trying to guess our astrological signs. She thought I was a Libra and that Carly was a Cancer. But I'm a Pisces and Carly is a Libra, so she was totally mixed-up. She still thought __we__ were wrong, not her.

↑ Julia — she's like a mother hen, always trying to make sure everyone's okay.

You're __sure__ you're not a Libra? Maybe you're on the CUSP or your moon is in that house. You have a lot of Libra energy.

← I thought she was going to SMELL me to see what my aroma revealed about me.

↑ Crystal

↑ Bianca — she's a master of tricks. She promises she'll teach us how to short-sheet a bed.

Jolene is the complete opposite. She's studying to be an engineer, so she knows a lot of stuff about science and machines. She and Crystal tease each other that Jolene can teach us useful things like knot-tying, starting a fire, using a compass, and Crystal can show us the constellations and how to make scented candles and tie-dye shirts. They're a good combination.

↑ Paige - she's a little home-sick, but Bianca's her best friend, so she's okay.

Amrita — she's bossy, but Jolene's great at handling her and keeping her from controlling everything.

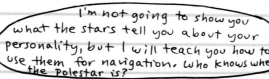

I'm not going to show you what the stars tell you about your personality, but I will teach you how to use them for navigation. Who knows where the Polestar is?

Jolene ↑

Yumi — she's a HUGE Harry Potter fan and brought all the books to reread at camp!

I'm beginning to think camp will be fun after all, even if Cleo is here — somewhere. The counselor-in-training group is pretty separate. They even eat at different times, so I haven't seen Cleo since we got off the bus. Sometimes I think I hear her distinctive guffaw-laugh, but when I turn to look, it's never her, just some other kid with a laugh like Cleo's. (Poor kid!) Carly keeps telling me to forget about my sister. I'm trying, really I am.

Carly is already deep into the camp experience. → She says she has 3 goals for the end of our time here.

1. To make a bull's-eye in archery.
2. To swim all the way across the lake.
3. To be named editor of the camp newspaper.

Carly impresses me because she knows herself really well. I mean, she knows what she wants, what she's good at, and what she needs to work on to get where she wants to be. Sometimes those things aren't so clear for me — like I think I want something, but when I get it, it turns out I didn't <u>really</u> want it after all. Or I think I'm good at something when I'm not, I'm just average. Or I think I'm a complete failure at something when I'm actually pretty good, I just have to try hard to succeed.

I'd like the same 3 goals as Carly except I don't want to be newspaper editor. Instead I'd like to be a staff cartoonist. And I'd like to make a bull's-eye, but I admit that's probably not going to happen, so I need a more reachable goal — like hitting the target at all.

I can imagine all the arrows whizzing past the target, hitting nothing but air. I'd like to hear the satisfying FWOOSH! "thwunk" as the arrow bites into the target — that's all I ask.

SWOOSH!

THWUD!

Our first night we stayed up late singing around the campfire (not at all annoying the way bus-singing is). It wasn't just our cabin, but all ten cabins in our group. That's a lot of kids, so it was a BIG campfire! I loved smelling the smoke, watching the flames crackle and pop, and picking out the constellations in the black, black sky — way darker than the sky ever gets at home. I would never admit it to Mom, but it was FUN.

There were so many stars, it was like a giant dot-to-dot in the sky. I found all kinds of amazing, new constellations.

The Giant Jelly-Roll Nose — watch out! It's gonna blow!

↑ The Heavenly marshmallow, get ready to toast!

The Big Mosquito — quick, get the Bug-Off!

↑ The Flying Canoe — now I just need to find the Celestial Paddle.

The Starry Poison Oak — whatever you do, DON'T TOUCH IT! →

me ↘

Carly ↙

I didn't sleep too badly considering the noise of several people snoring, the occasional whispers and farts (PU!), and the paper-thin mattress I slept on. I could face the chilly bathroom with all the big spiders in the corners. I could handle washing my face with cold water and listening to eleven other girls brush their teeth, but breakfast was something else! Talk about bad manners — chewing with open mouths, slurping, and burping. It was like having Cleo at the table ALL AROUND ME!

And then there was the food itself.

There's a scale of awful institutional food, from airplane meals to school cafeterias to camp food. Camp food is some of the best AND some of the worst.

BAD   CAMP   FOOD

soggy, canned green beans — never good ANYWHERE! ↙

barfy baked beans ↙

lumpy oatmeal ↓

watery hot chocolate ↑

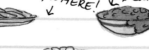

slimy lima beans ↖

No bean is a good bean unless it's a jelly bean! ↙

hobo stew — another name for leftover mush ↑

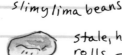

stale, hard rolls — nothing is fresh EVER! ↖

canned pineapple as if it's a treat ↖

The good camp food all has one essential ingredient that makes it taste great — a campfire. Anything cooked in, on, or over a campfire is DELICIOUS, especially if you eat it outside under a starry sky.

GOOD CAMP FOOD

banana boat
(dive in!)

Peel back one strip from the banana peel, slice off the top of the banana, put chocolate chips and mini marshmallows where you sliced, fold the peel back down, wrap in foil, and bake in the coals for ten minutes — yum!

pocket stew

Fill a piece of foil with chunks of potato, carrots, and peas, fold into a pouch, and set on a forked stick. Cook over the fire for half an hour, then munch!

walking soda — take an orange and roll it on a hard surface until it's all mushy. Take a peppermint stick, bite off both ends, then poke it into the orange. Use the peppermint stick as a straw to suck up the juice.

Pocket peach pie — sprinkle cinnamon and sugar on a peeled peach. Wrap in foil and bake in coals for twenty minutes — ta da! Dessert!

And of course, there's alway s'mores!

↑Add peanut butter   or caramel sauce

or make the classic version — the essential camp food! Have s'more!

Kayla seems a little better today, not quite so homesick, or maybe she's too exhausted to miss anyone now because we went on a looooooooong hike. I feel like my blisters have blisters! Our reward for so much exercise was to get the afternoon free for whatever we wanted. Most kids went right to the lake. That's what I wanted to do too, but Carly had other plans. She wanted to sign up right away to work on the camp newspaper, quick, before all the jobs were taken. I said there was no rush, it's summer, who wants to do extra work, but when Carly gets an idea like that, there's no talking her out of it.

I dreamed of floating on a raft. Carly dreamed of being an ace reporter.
↓

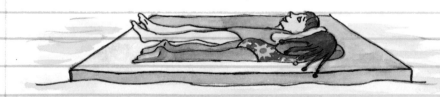

She's my best friend, so even though the cool, crystal clear water was calling to me, I went with her to the cafeteria where all the newspaper wanna-bes were meeting.

I thought there would be just a couple of kids, but there was almost a dozen, plus one camp counselor, Jeff, who's in charge of the newspaper.

Jeff had a long ponytail, a moustache, and a goatee, as if he couldn't get enough hair — he needed more, wherever he could grow it.

I think of reporters as high energy, aggressive type people, but Jeff was calm and soft-spoken. There was nothing urgent about him at all. I couldn't imagine him yelling, "Stop the presses! This is page one stuff!" Or even "Extra, extra, read all about it!"

It's good to see so many of you turn out for this meeting. Together we can put out a great little newspaper — and have fun while we're doing it.

After a short introduction about the newspaper (how many pages, how often it comes out, what it covers), Jeff divided up the jobs that needed doing. Then he passed around a piece of paper and asked us to sign up for our first three preferences.

*answers: 2 pages, once a week, camp news

Carly wanted to list hers as 1) editor, 2) editor, and 3) editor, but she knew that wasn't what Jeff meant by three choices. So she wrote down 1) editor, 2) columnist, and 3) reporter.

"What's the difference between a reporter and a columnist?" I asked. I should know this since my dad works for a newspaper, but I don't even know which one he is or what he does exactly.

"A columnist writes short essays about their opinions, like I could do a column on what makes a good name for a camp and what doesn't. A reporter writes about things that happen — newsworthy things, like who won the s'more-eating contest or how a skunk sprayed Cabin 6." Carly really knows her stuff.

You should interview me for my side of the story.

caramel

There could be a feature article about how to make the best s'mores next to the story about the s'more-eating contest. The same reporter could write both. Then the columnist could write about her personal search for the ideal s'more. It would be an all-s'more issue!

peanut butter

whipped cream

Add caramel or peanut butter or whipped cream — or all three — for more of a s'more!

I like the idea of being a reporter or a columnist, but my first choice is to be a cartoonist. I'd love to do a weekly strip. I know it can be a lot of pressure coming up with funny things to write about every week, but for the six weeks of camp, it's not that much, only six comics. I can do that. So I put down my choices as 1) cartoonist, 2) columnist, 3) reporter. I wondered what the other kids chose.

There was a group of boys who were good friends ↙

There was a boy who doodled the whole meeting. ↙

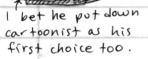

I bet he put down cartoonist as his first choice too.

There was a girl ↑ who was very bossy. (I'm SO glad she's not in our cabin!) She interrupted Jeff constantly, talking about what she did last year in journalism class. I can tell she wants to be editor and tell everyone else what to do.

↑ Whatever they do, they'll want to do it together, so I'm guessing they'll be reporters or maybe work on page layout as a team.

Listen to me!

Jeff said we'd know our positions by the end of the day. He's going to post them by the cafeteria door. Then the meeting was over.

And there was a girl who thought she was Ms. Star Reporter. The less said about her, the better!

Carly was excited about the meeting.
↓

This is going to be great — our own little newspaper! All ours!

Yes, and the best part is we can still go to the lake. C'mon, let's go swimming!

I was excited that it was over so soon.
↓

Okay, okay. I got my dose of journalism for the day, you can get your relaxation time.

After all, it IS summer, remember? Journalism is WORK!

The lake was as wonderful as I thought it would be. The water was so clear, you could see the bottom. I don't like swimming in dark water — that's kind of creepy.

I can't help imagining some giant fish is going to bite me when the water's too black to see in. Or if there isn't a fish, there'll be an evil eel which is even worse!

But this water was perfect — not too hot, not too cold, crisp and clear. There was a raft floating in the middle of the lake that was the perfect place to relax in the sun.

Carly and I stretched out and watched ↓ the other swimmers.

It was a wonderful, lazy summer day, almost like not being in camp at all.

"There's that boy who was at the newspaper meeting." Carly pointed to a kid diving from a rock.

"He's a good diver," I said. "I bet he ends up being a cartoonist for the paper."

"Why do you say that?" Carly asked.

"He was drawing the whole meeting. Kind of like me."

Carly gave me a look — a strange look, one I'd never seen on her face before and I couldn't tell what it meant. She seemed annoyed at me but I hadn't done anything, said anything, to bug her. I didn't get it.

"Is something the matter?" I asked.

"No! Why should something be the matter?" That's what she said, but her tone said yes, something's bugging me. "I'll race you back to the shore," she challenged. She didn't wait for an answer — she dived right in.

Talk about changing the subject! I jumped in after her and swam as fast as I could, but she still beat me.

I forgot about the boy until dinner when I saw the list Jeff had posted with the newspaper jobs. Carly didn't get to be editor-in-chief, but she is a columnist. I got my first choice — cartoonist. And so did the boy, just like I guessed. Now I know his name — it's Luke.

We all checked the list at the same time.

↓

Yay! I get to be a cartoonist!

Hey, me too!

Oh yeah, I see your name — Luke, right?

At least I got my second choice. Who's editor? Who is this Mike person?

I told Carly she should be happy — she's the only columnist. There are several reporters, one photographer, a couple of layout, design people, one editor, and two cartoonists. For such a small newspaper, it's a pretty big staff.

But Carly wasn't happy.
↓

It should be MY staff. I should be in charge.

I bet Jeff picked Mike because he's a boy — that's so sexist!

I thought maybe Carly was right — she didn't get the job because she's a girl. But the next day we had another meeting and I could see why Mike was made editor. He has a <u>lot</u> of journalism experience. Plus he's a nice guy, not the kind of person you can stay mad at. And he's cute — that makes it even harder to hold a grudge.

↑
The star reporter girl was upset that she's not the ONLY reporter. She wanted at least the title "Lead Reporter." All she gets is "reporter." I wish she'd stop whining about how she was cheated!

Even Carly had to admit that he was a good choice.
↓

Okay, people, we have a lot of work to do and not much time. Let's put out a paper!

We went on a really long hike today and Carly talked about ideas for her column the whole time. I love Carly. She's my best friend, but by the end of the afternoon I wasn't sure which was more exhausting — walking or listening to her.

My feet were so sore, it felt like my blisters had blisters.

My ears were even more sore. They were red and achy from the weight of so many words.

blah, blah, blah

I felt like the words were leaking out of my ears, there were so many of them crammed in there.

blah, blah, blah, blah

But Carly wasn't at all tired. She was still talking.

Maybe I should write an article on surviving long hikes, what to bring, that kind of thing...

...or I could write about my views on arts and crafts, which are the most crafty...

...or I could do a collection of camp songs — that'd be fun...

ENOUGH ALREADY!

Write about ANYTHING!

Write about EVERYTHING!

Just DON'T talk about it first!

"Well," Carly said, "aren't you grumpy! I was only trying to have a conversation about my column. I thought you'd <u>want</u> to talk about it since you're my friend."

"Yes, I'm your friend." I was exasperated. "But that wasn't a conversation. It was a long monologue you were having with yourself. I just happened to be nearby."

Carly laughed. It's a good thing she has a sense of humor or she'd be furious with me.

"You're right," she admitted. "I was really thinking out loud. It's just that I'm excited to have a column. I really want it to be great."

"And it will be," I said. "Now I need to work on my cartoon. I have to come up with some ideas too, you know. And mine have to be funny."

So while Carly worked on her column, I got started on my comic strip. I didn't even know who I wanted my characters to be. I had a <u>lot</u> of work to do.

possible comic strips
↓

I know, I know - it's BAAAAAD!

Why are all my characters food? Why are all my stories about being eaten? Maybe I need a snack.

Those were terrible. I needed a theme, like camp letters home or campfire stories or camp gossip. I decided to go for a walk to get some inspiration — a walk around camp, <u>not</u> a hike.

I found Luke down by the lake, sketching his own comic. I asked him if I could see, and he said sure.

It was a comic strip with foxes as the main characters, only they were at camp, like us.

WHAT ARE YOU MAKING YOUR LANYARD FOR?

YOU DON'T MAKE LANYARDS FOR ANYTHING. THEY'RE A ZEN ACTIVITY, A FORM OF MEDITATION.

WHAT ARE YOU MAKING A LANYARD FOR?

IT'S A ZEN THING, A MEDITATION. OH, FORGET IT— IT'S FOR MY BACKPACK.

COOL.

It was really good. I told Luke how much I liked it, and how I hadn't even started mine yet. We talked about how hard it is to get ideas and make them come out the way you want them to. We talked about comic book artists we like and don't like and why. We talked for so long, the dinner gong rang and I still hadn't done my comic. It was so easy to talk to Luke, I almost forgot he was a cute boy. He was something even better now — a friend.

We walked back to the cafeteria together and it all felt so normal and comfortable.

↓

↑

Until Carly saw us.

Then it suddenly felt strained and awkward and totally uncomfortable.

Carly almost looked like she was mad, but trying hard not to look it. →

There you are! I've been looking for you, Amelia. I thought you were working on your comic.

I guess not.

"I _was_ working on it," I explained. "Then I ran into Luke. He's already finished his comic — it's great."

Luke smiled. "I hope Mike thinks so."

Carly flashed a big smile. Suddenly she was super friendly, only not to me, to Luke.

"Oh, I'm sure Mike will," she cooed. "I think he's a good editor, don't you? He _really_ helped give me direction for my column. I'm writing a column, you know."

"Yeah," Luke nodded. "How's it going?"

Carly's smile grew even bigger. "How sweet of you to ask! Want to eat dinner with me and I can tell you about it?"

"Sure," Luke said, and they both headed for the line to pick up a tray.

I followed behind, acting like I was part of their

group, only I wasn't. Carly shut me out — my best friend!

They chatted all through the line as they picked up enchiladas, beans, and rice. Neither of them said anything to me — not one word. Then Carly led the way to a table that conveniently only had two seats left.

"Oh, sorry, Amelia." She turned to me. "I guess you'll have to find another table."

"Yeah," I said slowly. "I guess I do." I sat next to Kayla, feeling like steam was coming out of my ears.

I was so mad, I bit into my food like it was an enemy.

I chewed furiously. I didn't know you could chew angrily, but you can. Nothing tastes good, but it's satisfying to gnash and mash.

"What's wrong?" Kayla asked. "Are you homesick too?" She sniffled. "I talked to my mom today and I feel much better."

"Good for you," I snapped.

"Well, you don't have to be mean about it," said Kayla. "I'm just trying to be friendly."

"You're right — I'm sorry." I felt bad. It wasn't her fault that Carly was being so mean. "I had a fight with my best friend, so I'm not exactly in a friendly mood."

"Oh," said Kayla. There was a long pause. "Well, at least you're not homesick."

But I was homesick, homesick for Carly. I watched her laughing and talking with Luke and I missed her. She should have been doing that with _me_. I liked Luke, but I didn't like him taking Carly away. And I didn't like Carly taking Luke away — after all, _I_ was talking to him first.

The more I watched them, the more jealous I got. Only I wasn't sure who I was jealous of — Luke or Carly.

I wanted both of them to my friends, not each other!

They looked so happy together, it made me feel worse.

When I left the cafeteria, they were still talking.
I went back to the cabin and tried to work on my
comic. I didn't get anything made except for a big pile of
crumpled-up papers, all comic rejects.

↓

I had already washed up and brushed my teeth by
the time Carly got back. I was in a black, black
mood, and she looked so happy she was practically
floating.

"Isn't Luke perfect?" she burst in. "He's so sweet
and smart and funny. And cute, so cute!"

"Yeah," I said, "adorable. So adorable you dropped
me. That's a horrible way to treat a friend. You
like a boy, so suddenly I'm invisible?"

"I did that?" Carly looked startled, then
guilty. "I guess I did. Oh, Amelia, I'm sorry. It's
just that I really, really like him."

I wasn't letting her off the hook yet. "Yeah,
I can see that. Everyone can see that. But
does that mean you can treat me so badly, like
you barely know me?"

"You're right, Amelia, and I said I was sorry." Carly sounded grouchy. Maybe I'd pushed too hard, but a simple "I'm sorry" didn't feel like enough. I'd come all this way to this stupid camp to be with my best friend, not to have her dump me so she could be with a boy, especially a boy who was MY friend first.

We went to bed mad at each other. It felt terrible. I couldn't fall asleep for a long time and when I did, I had a nightmare.

Carly and Luke were whispering to each other and walking like they were glued together.

They walked right by me.

I said hi, but they ignored me. I felt invisible.

Then it got worse — they started kissing in front of me like I wasn't there. "Stop it!" I yelled. "Stop it NOW!"

But it didn't matter how loud I screamed. They kept on kissing and my throat got redder and sorer. I wanted to shove them apart, but I couldn't move. It was that horrible dream sensation of your feet being stuck in mud and there's no way to free them.

Finally, I was so exhausted, I collapsed on the ground and started to cry. There were no more screams left inside of me, just tears.

Then I woke up and I was really crying. My pillow was wet from tears.

I felt stupid crying in my sleep. →

And I felt sad— very, very sad. ↙

I can't lose Carly, I told myself. I'm not going to let a boy ruin our friendship. She can have Luke as a boyfriend — I don't care about that — but she has to keep me as a best friend, no matter what.

Once I decided that, I could go back to sleep and this time, I didn't dream anything. When I woke up, the first thing I did was talk to Carly.

I'm sorry I was mad at you yesterday. It's just that you're really important to me. I don't want a boy to come between us.

I don't want that either. We're too good of friends for that. But c'mon, Amelia, you can't be jealous of a boyfriend — if that's what Luke becomes. We have to agree that it's okay for each of us to have boyfriends, so long as we don't let them get in the way of _our_ friendship.

I agree! That's exactly what I want — our friendship comes first.

It was a beautiful, sunny morning, even sunnier because Carly and I were friends again. Breakfast is normally the worst meal at camp (no campfire, no starry skies), but even that was great today. Carly didn't even glance around to find Luke in the dining hall (like I did). We ate together as if we'd never fought.

The squirrels begging for food by the windows gave us each a good idea of what to do for the newspaper. Squirrels are furry and cute, but the counselors say we should NEVER feed them. They're not pets, they say, they're wild animals.

So that's what Carly and I are going to do, each in our own way — Pet Peeves and Pet Loves. Carly is going to interview kids and do a column on what people like and hate about camp, a kind of quick top ten list of each.

I'm doing the same thing, only as a comic strip and it's my own list, not other people's. We're going to ask Mike about having both things next to each other on the page.

I love it that Carly and I are more than just friends — that we can work together like this and inspire each other. We give each other our best ideas.

The finished version was smaller and neater, so it looked more like a comic.

Except there weren't many speech bubbles, so it was a ← free-form kind of thing.

Carly said it looked like a page out of my notebook. I guess that's the easiest way for me to think and draw.

Carly's column was really funny. I thought our pieces worked great together.

I really believed that. I didn't see any reason Carly couldn't have her little crush on Luke and still treat me like her best friend.

Then we had the newspaper party.

It wasn't really a party — it was a dinner where we all worked putting the paper together. We ate pizza, did final edits, played around with page layouts, then printed out the finished newspaper. It was a LOT of work and by the time it was over, we were all silly from being so tired.

Luke and I worked together on scanning and resizing our comics. We talked about our favorite comic websites and who the most interesting writers and artists are. The more we talked, the more I noticed how cute he was, how sweet and smart and sensitive. I was beginning to wish he was more than a friend. I mean, I really liked him — "like" like, not just like. And I wondered, did he like me?

The bossy girl who didn't get to be editor wasn't bad after all. She worked HARD!

Way more than ms. Star Reporter who just whined.

She said her talents were being wasted. What talent, I wondered.

I couldn't help it — I found myself staring at him. →

← Then I thought, is this what Carly feels? She can't like him this way. I want him to like me, not her.

Carly was busy with Mike most of the time but every now and then, I saw her looking in our direction and she didn't look happy. Once she even shook her finger at me and mouthed "What are you doing?" At least, I think that's what she was saying — that or "Cock-a-doodle-doo." I just shrugged my shoulders.

When she was finished, Carly came over to us, only she wasn't the Carly I knew at all. She was all fake smiles, tilting her head to the side, even her voice was different, all sugary and soft.

Jeff went from kid to kid, encouraging everyone to do their best work. Maybe that's what turned Carly into a major flirt. She was working it, alright!

I love your comic, Luke! It's the best part of the whole newspaper!

I swear, she was practically batting her eyelashes! I thought that only happened in cartoons.

That's sweet of you to say, but I think Amelia's comic is way better than mine. I laughed out loud when I read it!

I wanted to jump up and hug him! Not only was Luke NOT falling for Carly's nicey-niceness, he said good things about me — ME! That proved he liked me _better_. I glared at Carly. "See!" my eyes said. She glared back. "Oh, yeah?!" her eyes replied.

We gave each other the evil eye while trying to seem normal and friendly, so Luke wouldn't suspect anything. It wasn't easy. In fact, it was awful, but I couldn't leave because I wanted to be with Luke —and that was wonderful and magical. Finally the paper was put to bed (that's finished in newspaper talk) and we all had to go to bed ourselves.

Luke smiled and said good night to both of us. I smiled at him. Carly smiled at him. Then we glared at each other.

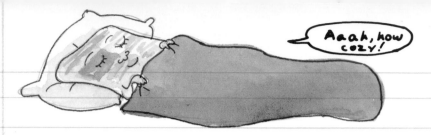

Aaah, how cozy!

I have a feeling ↑ only the newspaper slept well that night.

Carly and I didn't say anything as we walked back to our cabin until right before we got to the door. Then Carly exploded.

"How could you? You <u>know</u> I like Luke, we agree that it's okay that I like him, and then you go and flirt with him? What kind of friend ARE you?"

"Hey!" I snapped back. "I wasn't flirting — I was being friendly. I can't help it if Luke likes me. I didn't even think of him that way until <u>he</u> started flirting with <u>me</u>!"

"You are so full of it!" Carly's voice was hard and cold. "You like him — admit it! You like him!"

"Okay, I admit it." I tried not to yell. I didn't want the whole camp to hear us. "But I didn't <u>plan</u> on liking him. It just happened. It's not like I can turn my feelings off and on. And he did start it — not me. Besides, why can't we both like him?"

"Because we <u>can't</u>! Because that's not how friends treat each other. Because it's a betrayal!"

We stood outside the cabin, fighting in harsh whispers.

"I'm not betraying you! Can't we just leave it to Luke to pick who he likes more? I promise if he chooses you, I'll be fine with it. I'll still be your friend, no matter what." That's what I said, but I'm not sure I meant it. Anyway, I was certain Luke would choose me — we had so much in common, it was so easy to talk with each other. What would he and Carly talk about? It's true Carly was more cool than me. Maybe she was prettier — okay she _was_ prettier. But I was still confident that Luke liked me. I could just tell.

Okay, it's a deal then. We'll leave it up to Luke.

And we agree that we'll stay friends, no matter who he picks. No being a sore loser.

Carly seemed just as sure that Luke liked her best.

That got me thinking — how do you know if someone likes you? According to the movies, there are some obvious clues.

SIGNS OF A CRUSH

① Making moony goo-goo eyes at someone.

② Not being able to look someone in the face.

③ Stammering.

④ Laughing too long and too hard at someone's jokes.

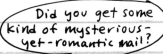

⑤ Sending anonymous love notes.

⑥ Always managing to be near the person.

I'm not sure those are really accurate. They seem so Hollywood pat, so prepackaged and sugary. I think the hints are much more subtle and you have to be very observant to catch them. I have my own list of how to interpret body language.

amelia's

SIGNS OF A CRUSH

He's not bored— he's in love!

① A slightly flared nostril — the passion can't help but escape.

With just the tiniest hint of a smile.

② A raised eyebrow at just the right moment.

Add the moony eyes and it's totally obvious!

③ A smile that lasts a second too long.

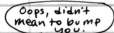

Oops, didn't mean to bump you.

④ Accidentally on-purpose touching.

⑤ Standing a smidgeon closer than normal.

Nice job.

⑥ Casual-yet-on-purpose-with-no-apologies touching.

The next few days I tried to read Luke like a book to see if he really did like me. It was exhausting! Sometimes he'd smile at me a certain way and I'd know he liked me, but later I'd see him smile kind of the same way at Carly or Jeff or Mike. Then I didn't know what to think.

Once he touched my arm, but he did that to Luis too when they were working on page layout together. Then he winked at me one night by the campfire and I was sure that meant something until the next morning when I saw him wink at the hairnet lady in the cafeteria — obviously he doesn't have a crush on her.

You want some bacon with that, dahlin'?

Maybe a nice sausage or two?

Maybe he was just trying to be nice so he could get an extra portion of bacon or something. Or does he flirt with EVERYONE? I was beginning to wonder.

Who knew having a crush could be so tiring! What made it all the harder was that I didn't have Carly to talk to and get advice from. We weren't fighting anymore but that was because we were **barely** speaking to each other. It was terrible. She was right there, in the same cabin, on the same hikes, getting the same bug bites and blisters, singing the **same** camp songs but she might as well have been a million miles away. I saw her everyday and still I missed her.

We'd said we'd be friends no matter what.

But that wasn't what was happening.

It was strange. I began to look at Carly the same way I watched Luke, examining her for any sign that she wasn't mad at me anymore and was ready to be my friend again. Once she smiled and waved to me from the raft on the lake and I was _so_ excited and happy until I realized she was waving to someone else.

I decided to talk to Carly about it. I wasn't so sure anymore about Luke, but I was certain about her — I knew we could be good friends. And I knew she liked me when we weren't both competing for the same boy.

"Carly," I said, "this is getting silly. We agreed we'd be friends no matter what, no matter who Luke picks, but we're not acting like friends."

"I'm not being unfriendly!" she snapped. "You're the one who's so standoffish."

"I am not!" I protested. "Or if I am, it's because you are."

"Well, that's a circular argument," Carly said.

She was right. We were like a dog chasing its tail! →

We were going around and around in a circle, never getting anywhere. ←

"You're right," I admitted. "And I'm breaking the circle right now. I want us to be friends." I tried to soften my voice, to sound nice and warm. "So, what are you doing for your next column?"

The chill in Carly's eyes thawed. "Well," she began, "I'm thinking about doing a spoof on a gossip column, like camp romances,

sightings of Bigfoot, that kind of thing."

"That sounds great," I said. And it did. Carly's full of good ideas. "I was going to do a comic on knot tying. There's something funny there, I'm just not sure what. Maybe how not to

knot. Or all the funny knot names."

↑
Bigfoot-
never actually
seen.

Carly nodded. It was such a relief to be talking with her again, to be normal with each other, the way we used to be.

We stood in the dark night, feeling better about each other, about everything. I didn't

want to go into the light of the cabin and break the spell. Then we heard a rustling behind us. It was a skunk. At least it had a skunk's body and tail, but the head was stuck in a yogurt container. It couldn't

↑
Camp Bear-
last sighted
in 1963.

Lake Ghost-
heard moaning
in 1972.
↓

see and was trying to shake off the container.

We froze, staring at the skunk. I was afraid that if we startled it by making any noise, it would spray us. For once I didn't need a guide on how to read someone's expression — I could tell Carly was thinking the exact same thing.

"What should we do?" I whispered.

"We have to help it," she whispered back.

I like skunks. They have cute faces and nice, fluffy tails, but I <u>don't</u> like the disgusting stink they spray and I was pretty sure that getting sprayed close up would be UNBEARABLE. You'd have that musky smell inside your mouth, ears, nose — you'd breathe it deep inside your lungs. Maybe it wouldn't kill you, but it'd be <u>MISERABLE</u>.

But the skunk looked even more miserable, trying desperately to get the plastic carton off its head. And if we didn't help it, it would die.

I stopped thinking, I stopped smelling. I stopped breathing. I just stepped forward, grabbed the yogurt container, and quickly pulled it off. Then I braced myself, waiting for the awful spray.

I waited with my eyes closed tight, but no horrible smell came. I opened my eyes and saw the skunk amble off into the bushes, like a tame cat or dog, not a potentially highly stinky skunk.

Carly grabbed my arm, laughing. "Did you see that? It didn't even say thank you!"

"Oh yes, it did," I said. "It didn't spray us, did it? I can't believe I dared to take off that container."

"I can't believe it either." Carly grinned.

And just like that, we were friends again. We didn't say anything about Luke. We didn't need to.

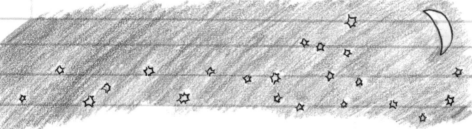

It was a beautiful night, crisp and clear. The stars sparkled in the sky and there was a new moon, pale and slender, a new beginning. It was so nice, I didn't even mind the bugs, the hard bunk bed, the smelly bathrooms, the dangerous skunks. I actually liked being at camp — for now. Which is good because there's still a couple weeks left to go.

That lasted a few days, until the dance was
announced. Then Carly and I were right back
where we started, wondering who Luke would pick,
who he would ask to go to the dance with him.

CAMP RUNAMUCKA
DANCE-A-MUCKA!
IT'S THE LAST NIGHT OF CAMP - GO WILD!

Actually this time, things weren't as bad between
us. We were still talking, even if a lot of the talk
was teasing about how Luke would never choose the
other person. The frosty anger was gone, melted
away by the skunk. Instead there was a competitive
edge — may the best girl win!
    Carly thought that was her and sometimes I agreed
with her. When she showed off at the lake, doing a
perfect dive from the raft, I saw how Luke admired
her. But I also saw how Luke liked my drawing, my sense
of humor.

That's as important as graceful dives and strong swimming, isn't it? At least, I hope it is.

I always try to sit next to Luke at the campfires, but I've only managed to get a chance twice. He's sat next to Carly a couple of times too, but he's also been by Kayla, Leanne, and Sara. I wonder if that means anything.

I was coming back from the bathroom last night when I overheard Crystal and Jolene talking. I didn't mean to snoop, but I couldn't help listening.

It's so cute how they're all excited about this dance. It reminds me of when I was in middle school.

Yeah, I always had these intense crushes on guys who wouldn't look twice at me. Good thing I wised up.

I dunno - I kind of liked the whole impossibility of liking someone who barely knew I existed. It was so romantic.

Romantic or pathetic?

You should talk! You're crazy about Jeff and he isn't interested in you at all!

He is so — I can tell! I bet he asks me to the dance.

He's not into you that way. Everyone can tell except you.

We'll see about that — when I'm dancing with him on Saturday!

I had no idea that Jolene had a crush on Jeff! And I didn't know that grown women like her and Crystal had as much trouble telling if a guy likes them as Carly and I do. No wonder I'm so confused — even experts don't know. So much for all the helpful clues on how to read men. For some things, there are no maps. You just have to stumble around blindly and hope for the best.

He loves me.

He loves me not.

He loves me.

The old daisy-plucking method was just as reliable.

I told Carly what the counselors said. After all, we're in the same boat, clueless about who Luke really likes better.

It was like old times. Carly curled up next to me and we whispered together, trying not to wake up anybody.

I do think he's going to ask me to the dance.

He almost did today, but then he got distracted by some kid from his cabin.

I mean, some things you know.

Or you think you know. I thought for sure he was going to ask me today too. Then Kayla started talking to him.

Who's right? Are Carly's instincts better than mine? Does anyone have a good sense about this stuff? What if Jolene really doesn't get it? What if none of us do? It's all a big mystery.

At least Carly and I can talk about this now. If I'm wrong and Luke doesn't like me that way, I'll still have Carly for a friend. I'll be sad and disappointed, but I won't be lonely.

I almost forgot that Cleo's here. Camp's almost over and I hadn't seen her at all until today. She and some of the other counselors-in-training were decorating the cafeteria for the dance tomorrow. The theme is a Hawaiian luau even though we're in the mountains.

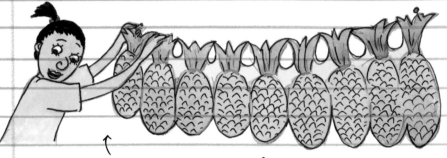

Cleo was hanging a banner of pineapples. She waved when she saw me.

"Hey, Amelia." Cleo sat next to me once she'd fixed her pineapples. "How are you liking camp? It's great, isn't it?"

"Yeah." I nodded. "It's good."

"You're going to the dance, aren't you? I'm going with Brendon." She nodded at a boy hanging paper parrots from the ceiling. "So who's y<u>ou</u>r boyfriend?"

"I don't have a boyfriend," I said. "I'm too young." I didn't want Cleo to know anything about Luke, but she was going to the dance too. She'd see everything.

"You don't need a date to go to the dance, you know," Cleo said. "Go anyway. It's gonna be a lot of fun. There's going to be a hula contest!"

I imagined Cleo wearing coconuts and a grass skirt. It wasn't a pretty picture.

Cleo, trying to be graceful...

...and keep the right rhythm at the same time - no easy task for her!

This dance was beginning to sound like the OPPOSITE of fun. Suddenly I didn't even want Luke to ask me because then I'd have to go and it would all be horribly embarrassing.

Cleo must have read my mind because she said, "Come on, Amelia, don't look like that! You don't have to hula- no one does. It's just to get into the spirit of things." She paused. "Don't worry, I'm not entering the hula contest. I promise I won't do anything to embarrass you."

"I'm not worried about that!" I lied. "It'll be great to see you at the dance."

"Good." Cleo nodded. "So what happened to Carly? Usually the two of you stick together but I saw her leave after dinner with some guy. So now she has a boyfriend?"

I could feel my cheeks get hot, though I tried not to blush. (Somehow trying not to look embarrassed only makes it worse.) "Luke's just a friend, not a boyfriend," I mumbled. "He's my friend too."

"Oh, I get it!" Cleo grinned. "You both like the same boy! That can be tough. I remember when that happened with Gigi and me. I swear, I almost clawed out that girl's eyes!"

I don't know why I thought Carly and I were the only friends with this problem. Of course this happened to other people. Of course friends survived this kind of thing all the time.

"So you and Gigi stayed friends?" I asked.

Yeah, we did. But she got the guy. I was sore for a while, but then I met someone else. And Gigi broke up with him anyway after a few weeks.

I mean, there's always another guy — no offense, Brendon — but there's only one Gigi! Guys come and go — she's forever.

I smiled. That sounded right. "Thanks, Cleo," I said and I meant it. For once I was glad she was around for me to talk to. She could even hula at the dance and I wouldn't mind.

I went to find Carly and told her what Cleo had said.

"Of course you'll always be my friend," Carly agreed. "But I have to tell you, I REALLY like Luke. I can tell you don't like him as much as I do, so why don't you just step out of the way? Isn't that what a true friend would do?"

I felt cornered. "How do YOU know how much I like Luke? Why should I bow out and not YOU? You're being so unfair — and selfish! You don't want a true friend — you want a doormat!"

It started out nice but it ended ugly. We were both furious and not speaking to each other — again.

↓

The next day was awful. Luke <u>still</u> hadn't asked me to the dance, but I could tell he hadn't asked Carly either. I decided to help him out a bit. Maybe he was just shy. I sat down next to him at lunch.

I waited for him to say more, to say "let's go together" or "want to come with me?" But he didn't. He just finished eating and said "See you later." See you later? That was it?

I put my head down on the table. It was time to admit that Luke would never ask me, that he didn't like me "that" way. Carly was right. He liked her better.

I heard someone sit down next to me. Had Luke come back? I looked up. It was Carly.

"You're right," she said. "He doesn't like me that way. He likes you. I'm sorry I yelled at you. I'm sorry I was such a selfish jerk." She sighed. "Have fun at the dance."

He hadn't asked Carly either? I shook my head. "Thanks for the apology, but Luke didn't ask me. I practically asked _him_, but he didn't take the hint."

Carly looked surprised. "Really?"

"Really," I said. "So how about we go to the dance together. And maybe Luke's just super shy and once he sees you there, he'll ask you to dance."

Carly rolled her eyes. "I'm not counting on that, but he might ask YOU. Either way, let's go and have fun."

I nodded. I have to admit that part of me was glad Luke hadn't asked Carly. That way I didn't feel so bad about him not asking me. Best of all, I had my friend back. Maybe no boyfriend, but still a best friend.

Hearts are complicated things. There's no explaining likes and dislikes, loves and hates.

When we got to the dance, Cleo was already there with Brendon, but there was no sign of Luke. Carly and I were eating cookies when we saw him walk in – WITH A DATE!

WITH KAYLA!

Carly and I just stared at each other.

We were stunned, flabbergasted, floored, astonished. Kayla, the whiny, homesick kid? When did Luke ever say he liked her? When had we seen them together? When had all this happened?

I have to give Carly credit. At first she was in shock. Then she was furious. She waited until Kayla went to the bathroom. Then she stormed over to confront Luke.

"I thought you liked _me_," she said. "I thought you were going to ask _me_ to go with you."

Luke paled. "I do like you, Carly," he said, "but not _that_ way. I never said I did."

"Not with words, no, but in other ways!" Carly insisted.

I could see the steam coming out of Carly's ears. I actually felt sorry for Luke. He was right about Carly being strong. She could flatten him like a steamroller if she wanted to. She could bury him in an avalanche of angry words and we'd have to send a search party to dig him out. Carly fumed. Luke looked terrified. I held my breath.

"Your loss, then." Carly bit off the words. She didn't yell. She calmly turned around, walked over to Mike, and asked him to dance. That girl had style!

You would think that after that, the dance would be ruined. But it wasn't. It was fun. Carly and I danced a lot, with a bunch of different boys and with each other. Now that we knew who Luke really liked, all the tension was gone.

The funny thing was, I wasn't even jealous watching Kayla and Luke together. Maybe I would have been if it had been Carly and Luke, but just knowing that Luke chose someone like Kayla over someone like Carly, that made me like him a lot less.

I'm not saying Kayla was a bad person, but she was clearly a project, someone who needing tending, like a plant. Luke didn't pick her because of who she was, but because he could feel strong next to her, because he thought he could rescue her and make himself a hero.

Cleo came over to Carly and me at the end of the dance. "You guys look like you had a good time," she said.

"We did." I smiled. I hoped she wouldn't say anything about us liking the same boy. Sometimes Cleo can be sensitive. Luckily she was this time.

"Me too," she said instead. "If my best friend had been here, it would have been perfect."

Carly and I looked at each other. "Yeah," Carly said, putting her arm around me. "We're pretty lucky."

We walked back to our cabin, stopping to look at the stars. →

It was a beautiful night. We heard an owl hooting and saw a shooting star and there were no skunks. It was perfect.

"You know, Carly," I said, "we're too young to have a boyfriend anyway, don't you think? We have all of high school to deal with that. Maybe middle school should be a boyfriend-free zone."

"Maybe," Carly agreed. "But we aren't in school now. What about summers? Isn't camp supposed to be a place where you can try new things and if they don't turn out the way you expected them to, it doesn't really matter because it's camp, not regular life?"

"Yeah, that's a good thing about camp," I said.

I wondered what risky things I'd done this summer that I wouldn't have dared to try at home. Canoeing? Rock climbing? Freeing a skunk from a yogurt container? Practically asking a boy to a dance (or strongly hinting at least)? All those were things that could only happen at camp.

"Shhh." Carly hushed me. "Look," she whispered.

On the bench near our cabin there were two people sitting close together. Really close. So close they were kissing.

"Hey!" I whispered. "It's Jolene and Jeff!"

Carly nodded. "At least _she_ was right about being liked."

I'll have to ask Jolene for _her_ list of signs of a crush before we leave tomorrow. I'm glad to know _somebody_ can get it right.

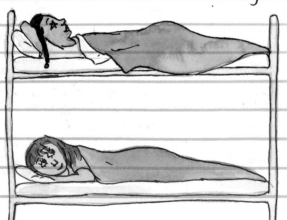

Finally, after _so_ long, the bunk bed felt comfortable and cozy. Just in time to go home.

←